Elizabeth Wellburn

ECHOES *from the* SQUARE

by ELIZABETH WELLBURN *with paintings by* DERYK HOUSTON

ECHOES *from the* SQUARE

by ELIZABETH WELLBURN *with paintings by* DERYK HOUSTON

Rubicon Publishing Inc.

Echoes from the Square
©1998, Rubicon Publishing Inc., Oakville, Ontario, Canada

ISBN 0-921156-99-5

Designed by Wycliffe Smith

Canadian Cataloguing in Publication Data
Wellburn, Elizabeth
Echoes from the square

ISBN: 0-921156-99-5

I. Houston, Deryk. II. Title.

PS8595.E5564E23 1998   jc813'.54   C98-930360-8
PZ7.W44Ec1998

98 99 00 01 02 5 4 3 2 1

Printed in Hong Kong

to our children

Here is a book that will introduce children to the moving story of Vedran Smailovic, a real present-day hero whose spirit I greatly admire. His spontaneous act of courage can be an inspiration to us all. It shows that an individual can make a difference in this world.

Yo-Yo Ma

In Appreciation

Long before I met Vedran Smailovic, his actions inspired me to write this story about his courage
and the love he shared through music in the midst of a devastating war. It was a great honour to
eventually meet him and an unforgettable joy to hear him play the cello. Mr. Smailovic also
became an important contributor of ideas and images that helped me to complete this book.
I thank him for reliving the tragic events that took place in Sarajevo, and for describing so vividly
the details that I would not have been able to imagine.

Elizabeth Wellburn

Not too long ago, this was a beautiful place.

Magnificent buildings stood around the cobblestone square. They had been there for hundreds of years. Trees lent their shade over benches placed by the streets. All around the square, pots brimmed over with colourful flowers. Everything was well-tended and loved.

A boy named Alen used to pass through this square every day with his friends. Alen liked to listen to the rhythm of footsteps and bicycle wheels clattering over the stones. In the background the murmur of people laughing and talking was gently muffled by the breeze and the birds singing in the trees. The air smelled clean. Alen loved coming to the square.

After school, Alen and his friends often stopped to buy cakes and pastries from a bakery nearby. While the other children lingered to play, Alen usually hurried off on his bicycle to a music class or rehearsal.

Not too long ago, this was a safe place. People greeted each other with smiles and exchanged stories and laughed together. Children darted about, busy with their games.

Then a day came when the grown-ups whispered about wars beginning in nearby cities. With worried looks, they said, "It could never happen here."

When they first heard the rumours, Alen's friends thought a war might be exciting. But Alen wondered if he could be brave if it ever happened. He cringed when his friends laughed and said, "You'll probably hide away somewhere with your violin and miss everything."

Now the war has come, and Alen knows there is nothing exciting about it.
Only horror and destruction.

Everything has changed. A cloak of darkness smothers the city.
Bombs and bullets fall like rain. Faces show the fearful expression of those
who must listen for every sound and watch around every corner.

Around the square, many buildings are in ruins. Every day yet another
pile of rubble appears where a building used to stand. Trees have been
cut down for firewood, the birds have flown away, and no flowers are to
be seen.

When Alen comes here, he almost chokes from the evil-smelling smoke
that never goes away. Even his bicycle has been destroyed.

It has been months since Alen has seen most of his friends. Some,
he knows, have been injured or killed. Many have left the city.
Schools are closed so children continue their lessons in shelters.

Each night in his cellar, Alen practises the violin. Sometimes his father
sits with him and listens. Alen's parents work long hours at the hospital,
and when they return they are weary and sad.

Alen wishes he could stay indoors, but there is no choice.

Every day, he must go outside to stand in line for water and carry it all the way home. If he doesn't do this, his family will have no water to drink or to use for washing.

Alen's heart pounds loudly with fear as he waits. When he is finally able to leave he can barely hear the beat of his own footsteps against the blasts of explosions and shootings.

Each step requires great caution, for just yesterday there had been a devastating bomb explosion nearby. Alen's heart is gripped in terror. He longs to move faster, to get home quickly, but there is rubble under his feet, his legs tremble, and he is weighed down by the heavy bottles of water.

Suddenly, he is startled by a sound, at first terrifying, and then strangely familiar. Could someone really be tuning a cello...here...now?

Alen turns the corner and is astonished. A man is sitting in a chair in the middle of the street calmly preparing to play a cello that he has unpacked from a worn-looking case. Alen shakes his head in disbelief.

"Who is that man? What is he up to?" he wonders as he hurries off, having been warned never to loiter here.

The music rises as Alen leaves, and he realizes that the stranger is a great musician. People appear in doorways and windows and watch in amazement.

For the first time in months, Alen walks past ruined buildings without thinking about bombs and snipers. Instead, his thoughts are with the cellist, and he wonders again, "Why is he making music in the street?"

Every day after that, Alen hurries through the square after fetching the water, wondering if he will see the cellist again.

Day after day, the man is in the square and his music soars above the broken cobblestones, touching the people who gather to listen.

Alen lingers for a few seconds longer each day. He knows he has to hurry on, but he is unable to pull himself away.

Alen can't stop looking at the cellist's face. The man's eyes are nearly closed, but Alen senses that he is seeing many things as he plays. People have gathered around to listen, and they hold each other and cry. Music fills their hearts and reminds them all of happier days. It stirs in them the hope that these forlorn times can pass.

One day, Alen stops and listens until the man has played the entire piece of music. He has forgotten to be afraid.

Walking home, Alen imagines the music as vividly as if the cellist was still playing beside him. He remembers a cherry tree laden with fruit that is nearly ready to pick, and he comes up with an idea.

Three weeks after the musician first appeared, Alen's father comes home early from work. Alen says to his father, "Papa, please come with me for the water today. I want you to meet the cellist I have been talking about."

After filling their bottles, Alen and his father walk to the square and listen until the cellist stops playing.

Then Alen's father approaches the cellist and says, "My son and I have enjoyed your music. Alen plays the violin and he wants to become a musician like you. We do not have much to offer, but we would like you to share a meal with us at our home."

In another time and place it might seem unusual to invite a stranger into your home, but a war can change many things.

"My name is Vedran," the man says. "I would be very happy to join you. Thank you."

They eat in the cellar, the safest place. It is a simple meal of homemade bread, lentil soup, and water. Alen has picked enough cherries to fill the largest bowl. The bright red fruits are sweet and juicy.

After the meal, Vedran looks up and begins to speak.

"Nothing starts with the present you know, Alen. The music I have been playing in the street these past weeks came from a man who lived long ago. His name was Albinoni and he wrote hundreds of beautiful pieces. Sadly, much of his music is gone because the only copies were kept in buildings that have been destroyed by wars.

"After one terrible war, a small fragment of a music script was found amongst broken stones and dust."

"Was it Albinoni's music?" Alen asks.

"Perhaps," says Vedran. *"We'll never know for sure."*

Then he continues, *"Only someone who loved the good things from the past could have dreamed of creating a whole piece of music from that simple scrap containing just a few notes. A man named Giazotto had this dream. He rebuilt Albinoni's music and created the beautiful "Adagio" that you have heard me play for the past 22 days."*

Vedran's voice now drops to a near whisper, every word is almost a sigh:

"Next to my house was the bakery. You probably remember the days before the war, when the bakery was full of many types of bread and rolls, cookies and cakes… it was not too long ago.

"It was morning, 23 days ago. By the bakery a long queue of people waited patiently and with dignity for a truck that would bring them bread. They waited for hours. They waited until late afternoon. Then suddenly, there was a terrible explosion… a shell had exploded… just steps away from them!

"In the first instant there was utter silence... shock... and then, chaos!... Fearful screams, yelling, shouting, blood.... People lay about... dead... and wounded. From my home I heard the cries for help. I dashed out and saw... intermingled masses of bodies... blood everywhere. Everyone was in shock. Some ran away, agony on their faces... some ran towards the massacre, trying to help the wounded. Then cars arrived with rescuers... to help those who were injured.

"Can you imagine, Alen, even some rescuers were hit by sniper fire. Finally, all the wounded people had been helped and the dead people taken away.

"Twenty-two people were killed in the blast."

As if coming back from a distant place, Vedran's voice slowly returns to normal.

"The whole town was filled with pain. I didn't sleep that night, wondering why this had happened to these innocent people, my good neighbours and friends.

"The next morning, I went out to look again… the area was adorned with flowers and wreaths. I had brought my cello, but I didn't know what to play. Tears just slid down my cheeks as I thought about the people who had died. I opened the cello case and somehow… something guided me to begin playing. Part way through, I recognized what I was playing — Albinoni's "Adagio." It had emerged as my musical prayer for peace.

"When I finished I noticed that people had stopped to listen and cry with me. As I talked with them I realized that this healing music helped us all to feel better. It provided us with hope.

"That was when I decided to play the same piece at the same place each day as a dedication to the 22 people who were killed in the bread queue. Today was my last day."

As if answering Alen's unasked question, Vedran continues to speak.

"I was afraid, I am still afraid. Everybody who's sane is afraid when there are bullets and shells in the air. But when I play, the darkness is lifted and I am able to show the world my other feelings. Music is love that connects people. My wish is for everybody to be able to share this."

Now Alen imagines a time when all the fear and grief will be over and rebuilding will begin. He picks up his violin and plays his favourite music, which echoes in the cellar. His eyes are nearly closed, but he sees many beautiful things.

When he finishes, he looks up at the smiling faces of his family and his new friend, Vedran.

They are sharing a dream and they know that one day music will be played again in this city, in peace and perfect harmony.

This book is a work of fiction, but it was inspired by the actions of Sarajevo cellist Vedran Smailovic, who also contributed to the ideas included.

Smailovic was born in Sarajevo, once a peaceful city in which people of different ethnic and religious backgrounds lived in harmony. In 1992, a tragic war began unfolding in Bosnia, which eventually led to a devastating seige of Sarajevo that lasted for one thousand days. During this time, Smailovic responded to the pain around him and helped the people keep their spirits alive by playing his cello in the streets of Sarajevo in the midst of continuing shelling and sniper fire.

Like thousands upon thousands of citizens, Smailovic eventually left Sarajevo because of the war. Currently living in Ireland, he has an ongoing commitment to war relief and performs many concerts each year to raise funds for war victims. Smailovic continues to create music and to help others, knowing that the ultimate defeat would be to give in to hatred or to wish for revenge.

Alen, the boy in the story, is a fictional character. He represents one of far too many children who have lost their lives or suffered the loss of loved ones, injury, malnutrition, and constant fear as a result of the war in Sarajevo.

Looking beyond Sarajevo, Alen represents one of millions of children who have been affected by recent conflicts and aggression around the world. Many of these children are now refugees, displaced from their homelands, and trying to rebuild their lives in unfamiliar surroundings.

Elizabeth Wellburn and Deryk Houston live in Victoria, British Columbia, Canada, with their two children, Amy and Samuel.

Elizabeth Wellburn is an educational researcher and has worked in the area of technology and distance education for over ten years.

Deryk Houston's art has been displayed in many solo and group exhibitions in Canada and the United States. In 1988, he was invited to represent the city of Vancouver in a solo exhibition in the (former) Soviet Union. Houston often donates his work to support charitable organizations in British Columbia.

Having first heard about Vedran Smailovic on the internet, Wellburn and Houston had the pleasure of meeting him in London, England, where they worked together on this book.

Website: http://coastnet.com/dhouston/